Belinda 🐾 AND THE Bears
and the
New Chair

Belinda 🐾 Bears
and the
New Chair

Kaye Umansky

Illustrated by
Chris Jevons

Orion
Children's Books

First published in Great Britain in 2015
by Orion Children's Books
an imprint of Hachette Children's Group,
a division of Hodder and Stoughton Ltd
Carmelite House
50 Victoria Embankment
London EC4Y 0DZ
An Hachette UK company

1 3 5 7 9 10 8 6 4 2

Text © Kaye Umansky 2015
Illustrations © Chris Jevons 2015

The paper and board used in this paperback are natural and
recyclable products made from wood grown in sustainable
forests. The manufacturing processes conform to the
environmental regulations of the country of origin.

A catalogue record for this book is available
from the British Library.

ISBN 978 1 4440 1351 1

Printed and bound in China

www.orionchildrensbooks.co.uk

For Freya, Elinor and Reuben

Contents

Chapter One

There were two cottages in Honeybear Lane. One had a door painted green.
 Behind that door lived Belinda, with her mum, dad and a cat called Gertie.

Behind the blue door lived...
The Three Bears!

The Three Bears were Belinda's new neighbours. They were shy and a bit worried about being the only bears in the village.

Belinda knocked on the Bears' door. She was being careful because she had an egg in her pocket. Today, she was planning to help the Bears bake a cake.

"Who's that?" came Daddy Bear's voice.

"Me," called Belinda. "Not that other girl."

PRIVATE!
LITTLE GIRLS NOT WELCOME.

Belinda knew better than to say the name. Goldilocks had brought the Three Bears bad luck.

She had eaten their porridge,

broken a chair

and made the sheets dirty with her muddy boots.

Shortly after Goldilocks' visit, the Bears' house in the woods had been knocked down to make way for a motorway. The Bears were trying to forget her.

The door opened and a delicious smell wafted out. Mummy Bear was making biscuits. Belinda was impressed. She hadn't known how to cook until Belinda had shown her.

Daddy Bear stood on the step.
He had a bandage on his right paw.

"What's wrong with your paw?"
asked Belinda.

"Nothing," growled Daddy Bear.

"Is that Belinda?" called
Mummy Bear. "Tell her to come and
have a biscuit."

"Go in," said Daddy Bear
grumpily. "Have a biscuit."

Without another word, he walked past Belinda, down the garden and into the shed. He shut the door.

Chapter Two

"What's wrong with Dad's paw?" asked Belinda, blowing on her biscuit.

Baby Bear bit into his. "Ow," he said. "H-h-hot."

"He hit it with a hammer," said Mummy Bear. "He's been trying to mend Baby's chair, but he's not good with his paws. He finds the nails fiddly. Why don't you take him a biscuit to cheer him up?"

"I will," said Belinda. She took a bite of her biscuit. "Yum. These are just right."

"Thanks to you," said Mummy Bear.

"When I come back, we'll make a cake," said Belinda. She took the egg from her pocket and gave it to Mummy Bear.

Belinda went down to the shed and knocked on the door.

"Me again," she called. "I've brought you a biscuit."

"I'm not hungry," said Daddy Bear.

Belinda pushed open the door.

Daddy Bear was staring down at a pile of splintered wood that once upon a time had been a chair. A little chair that had belonged to Baby Bear. The chair that had been just right – until Goldilocks had broken it.

"Oh dear," said Belinda.

""It's a mess," said Daddy Bear. He sighed. "Every time I try to fix it, I make it worse. But Baby must have a chair. He has to sit on a box. Bears need chairs not boxes."

"You could buy him a new one," said Belinda. "There's a furniture shop in town. You can go on the bus."

Daddy Bear shook his head.

"Oh, no, no, no. We're not ready for town yet. Or buses. Baby would be scared. It's all too new," he said.

Belinda thought Dad was using Baby Bear as an excuse. Belinda bet Baby would *love* to go on a bus.

"I'll think about it," said Belinda. "Mummy, Baby and me are going to bake a cake now. Do you want to help?"

"No," said Daddy Bear, sighing. "I'm just not in the mood."

Belinda, Mummy and Baby made the cake by themselves. They missed Daddy, but it was still huge fun!

"I have to go home now," said Belinda, when the cake was in the oven. "There's something I need to do."

She had had an idea.

Chapter Three

Belinda climbed the steps to her loft.

Belinda switched on her torch and shone it around. She was looking for something special. She knew it was here somewhere.

She could see cobwebs, her old pram, a broken lamp, more cobwebs, piles of magazines, boxes of books, a camp bed, Christmas decorations, Gertie's basket for when she went to the vet...

Ah! There it was!

Her very own high chair. It looked a bit old and shabby now, but she could easily fix that.

"Dad?" she called. "Can you help me get my old chair down, please? I need it for Baby Bear."

"Right you are, love," shouted her dad. He chuckled to himself. Baby Bear indeed! Belinda was always making up stories.

Chapter Four

"I've never seen anything like it!"
Daddy Bear was walking round and
round the high chair. "It's very *tall*,
isn't it? How would Baby climb up?"

"You can make it go lower,"
said Belinda. "You just pull this
little lever."

"How did you get it here?" asked
Daddy.

"In the wheelbarrow," said
Belinda. "I've brought some other
things too."

"Like what?" said Daddy Bear.

"Stuff we're going to need, to smarten it up," said Belinda.

"How?" asked Daddy Bear.

"We'll rub it down with sandpaper, so it's all smooth. Then paint it blue, like you did your front door," said Belinda.

"Mummy Bear did that," said Daddy Bear. "I'm no good with my paws."

"Painting's easy. When it's dry, we'll make it look lovely," said Belinda.

And that's just what they did.

They rubbed down.

They painted.

They waited for it to dry.

Belinda taught Daddy Bear a song about a Bear who went Over The Mountain.

They waited some more.

Daddy Bear told Belinda about
living in the Deep Woods.

They waited some more . . .
and sang . . . and talked . . .
Watching paint dry can be fun.

Chapter Five

In the kitchen, Mummy Bear and Baby Bear were gazing at the lovely cake cooling on the counter.

"Doesn't it smell nice?" said Mummy Bear. "I hope Belinda comes back soon to taste it. Go and call Dad, Baby. He'll want a slice."

Baby Bear ran to the shed. He knocked on the door.

"Dad?" called Baby. "Cake, Dad!"

"Baby?" came Belinda's voice. "Close your eyes. No peeping."

Baby closed his eyes. A hand reached out, took his paw and led him in. It was all very exciting!

"Now, open them," said Belinda.
Baby Bear opened his eyes.

"Surprise!" shouted Belinda and
Daddy Bear.

And there it was! The best ever Baby Bear chair in the whole wide world.

MY FIRST PICTURE BOOK

"What do you think?" asked
Daddy Bear. "Want to give it a try?"
Baby Bear walked up to his new
chair. He gave a balloon a gentle
poke. He smoothed the shiny ribbon
with his paw.

Then he climbed into the seat and wriggled to make himself comfy. He stared down at the book.

"It's a book," explained Belinda. "It's got pictures, see?"

Gently, Baby Bear turned to the first page.

"Bear," he shouted, pointing excitedly. "Like me."

"What's going on?" asked Mummy Bear from the doorway. Then –

"*Oohhhh*. It's wonderful."

Belinda smiled happily. Yes, she thought. It was just right.

Chapter Six

"Ready for your tea?" called Belinda's mum.

"Can I have it later?" asked Belinda. "I've just had some cake with the Bears."

"Was it nice cake?" asked her mum.

"Lovely. Mummy Bear's a good cook. Can I lend her a book of pudding recipes, please?"

"Of course," said her mum. "Tell her to try the trifle."

"How did Baby Bear like the chair?" asked her dad.

"He loved it," said Belinda. "Daddy Bear and I fixed it up. I taught him a song."

Her mum and dad exchanged a wink. Belinda and her stories!

That night, Belinda lay on her bed feeling very pleased with herself. The Three Bears were settling in nicely. Helping them was fun. They hadn't left their cottage yet. That would be the next thing to sort out. But for now, things were going well.

"Today was a big success, Gertie," said Belinda. "In fact, I don't know what those Bears would do without me."

THE SONG BELINDA
TAUGHT DADDY BEAR

The Bear went over the mountain,
The Bear went over the mountain,
The Bear went over the mountain,
To see what he could see,
To see what he could see,
To see what he could see.

But all he saw was the mountain,
The other side of the mountain,
All he saw was the mountain,
That's all that he could see.

THINGS TO SEE
IN THE DEEP WOODS

Fir cones

Conkers

Birds' nests

Wild flowers

Toadstools

What are you going to read next?

Have more adventures with Horrid Henry,

or save the day with Anthony Ant!

Become a superhero with Monstar,

float off to sea with Algy,